D1451152

A FISH IN
HIS POCKET

Denys Cazet

Orchard Books / New York / London

A DIVISION OF FRANKLIN WATTS, INC.

Orchard Books, 387 Park Avenue South, New York, NY 10016
Orchard Books Canada, 20 Torbay Road, Markham, Ontario 23P 1G6
Divisions of Franklin Watts, Inc.

Manufactured in the United States of America   10   9   8   7   6   5   4   3   2   1

The text of this book is set in 18 pt. Novarese Book.
The illustrations are pencil and watercolor drawings, reproduced in halftone

Library of Congress Cataloging-in-Publication Data
Cazet, Denys. A fish in his pocket.
Summary: all through school Russell is worried about the little orange fish in his
pocket, until he figures out how to return it to its pond.   [1. Fishes—Fiction.
2. Schools—Fiction]   I. Title. PZ7.C2985Fi   1987   [E]   87-5462
ISBN 0-531-05713-5   ISBN 0-531-08313-6 (lib. bdg.)

For Frances Keene,
with affection and gratitude

One November morning, Russell waved good-bye
to his mother and walked off to school.

He listened to someone playing the piano
as he walked along, and kept time to the music
with puffs of warm air.

He took a shortcut through a grove of shaggy trees.
They smelled like his grandmother's pantry.

When he reached Long Meadow Pond,
he stopped and broke the morning ice.
He looked into the water.
A school of little fish looked back.

Suddenly, Russell's arithmetic book
slipped out of his backpack
and fell into the pond.

He reached into the cold water
and pulled the soggy book out of the mud.
He felt cold all over.

Russell zipped up his jacket
and trudged on to school.

"My goodness," said the teacher. "What happened?"
"It was an accident," said Russell.

"Well," the teacher said, "accidents will happen. But, Russell, they won't happen often if we pay attention . . . if we take care."

The teacher oozed open the book. Some moss and a little fish slid to the porch floor.

"Oh my," the teacher sighed.

Russell picked up the little fish.
It didn't move.

"I didn't do it on purpose," Russell said,
following the teacher into school.

"I know," she said. "I can help you
take care of the arithmetic book,
but I don't know what to do about the fish."

"I don't know either," said Russell.

The teacher put the book next to the radiator.
Russell put the fish in his pocket.

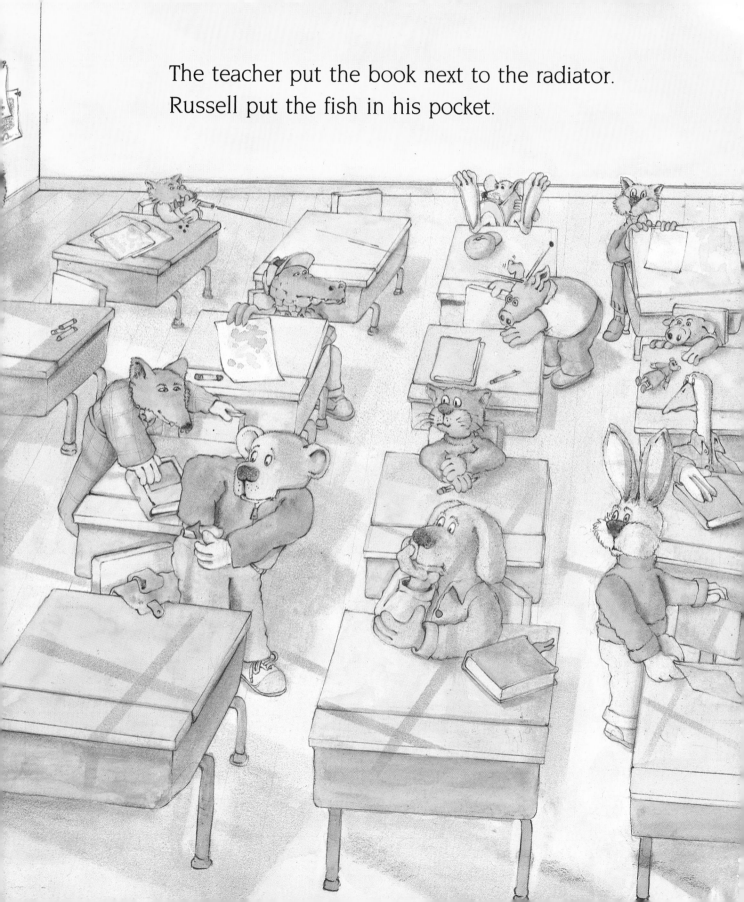

During reading, Russell lost his place.

At lunch time, he wasn't hungry.

During art, Russell couldn't think of what to draw.
He folded the paper in half, then folded it again . . .
and again . . . and again.

"I know!" shouted Russell, jumping out of his seat.

"Russell, please," said the teacher. "This is a quiet time."
"I know," he said softly.

After school, Russell ran to the pond.

He put his backpack on the ground
and looked into the water.
The school of little fish looked back.

Russell took out the folded paper and his pencil.
"All boats need a name," he said. "Take Care is yours."

He reached into his pocket and found the little fish.
He put it in the paper boat.

Russell set the boat on the water
and watched it sail away.
"Take care," he said.

Russell walked home under the shaggy trees
and into the warm November sun.

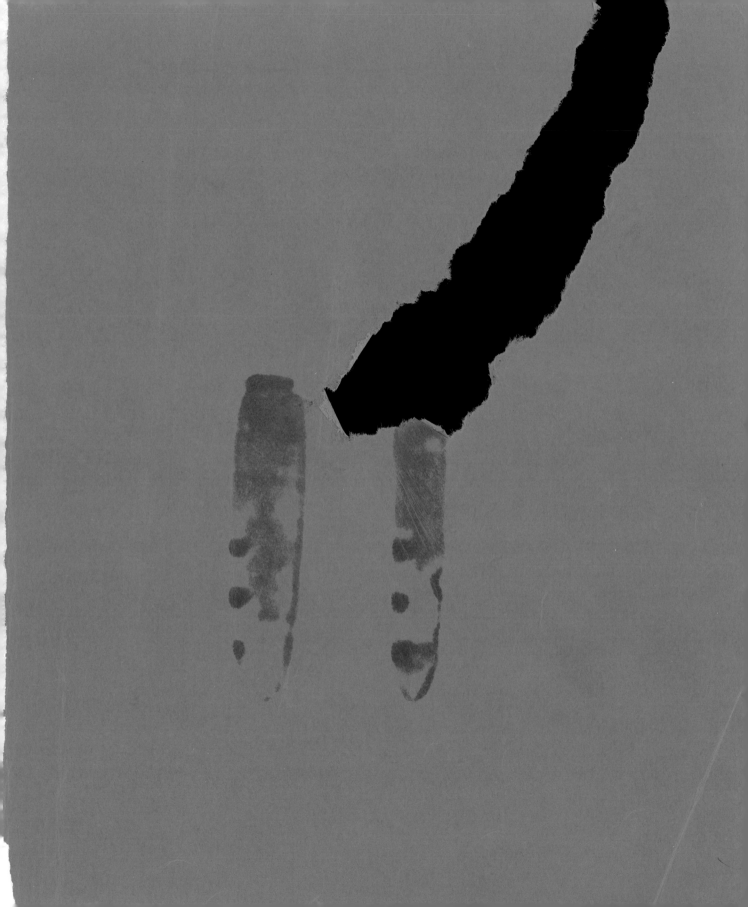

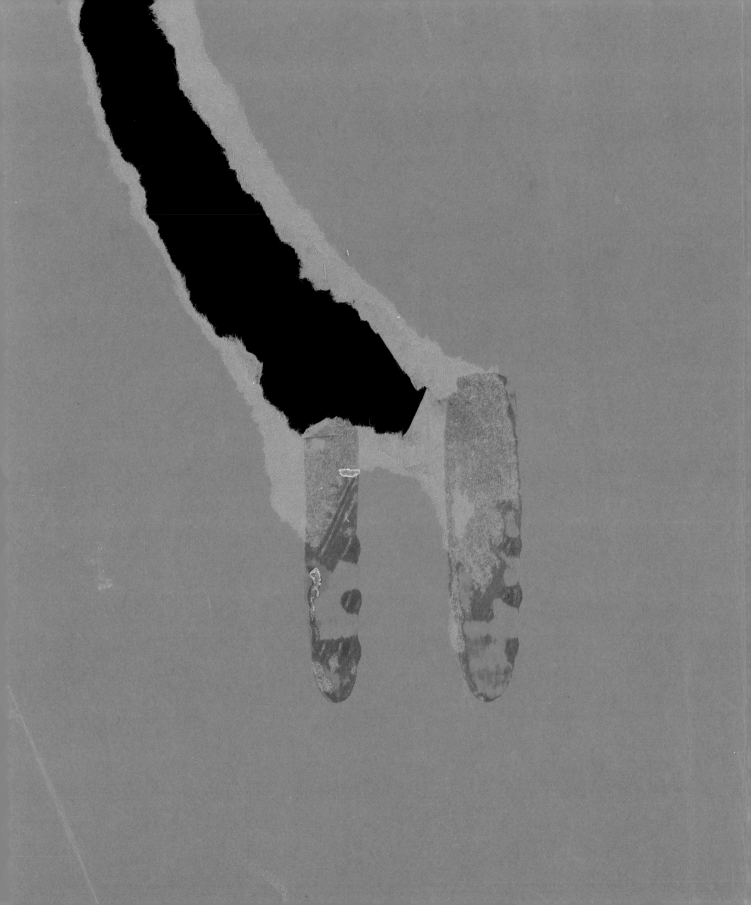